u y y o c k

This book belongs to
Ms. Zapf

LADY BORTON

FAT CHANCE!

ILLUSTRATED BY

DEBORAH KOGAN RAY

PHILOMEL BOOKS • NEW YORK

To Julie and Jess, Brooke and Chris —L.B.

To Barbara —D.K.R.

The artist used transparent watercolors to create the illustrations for this book.

Text copyright © 1993 by Lady Borton.   Illustrations copyright © 1993 by Deborah Kogan Ray.
Published by Philomel Books, a division of the Putnam & Grosset Group,
200 Madison Avenue, New York, NY 10016. All rights reserved.
This book, or parts thereof, may not be reproduced in any form without permission in writing from the publisher.
Published simultaneously in Canada.   Printed in Hong Kong by South China Printing Co., (1988) Ltd.
Book design by Gunta Alexander. The text is set in Holland Seminar.
Library of Congress Cataloging-in-Publication Data
Borton, Lady.   Fat chance! / by Lady Borton; illustrated by Deborah Kogan Ray.   p.   cm.
Summary: Marty Louise finds a blind stray cat and worries that her mother will not let her keep him.
[1. Cats—Fiction.]   I. Ray, Deborah Kogan, ill.   II. Title
PZ7.B648497Fat 1993 [E]—dc20 92-3339 CIP AC
ISBN 0-399-21963-3
1 3 5 7 9 10 8 6 4 2
First Impression

Keep Marty Louise home the rest of the school year," the doctor said. "The rheumatic fever might hurt her heart."

Marty didn't feel sick until the school bus stopped for Derek. Then, she felt her heart go hollow. Already Marty missed her friends.

"You can play with Wobbly Dog," Derek called. "If she'll let you."

"Wobbly," Marty said as soon as Derek left, "I'm in charge." Marty clicked her fingers to make Derek's *SNAP*. But Marty's fingers only went *whisp*.

Wobbly wouldn't play. She folded her tail away.

"You win, Wobbly," Marty said.

"Work on your letters, dear," Mom said.

Marty bristled. She hated letters. Letters were prickly, like porcupine quills. Letters had barbs all over, and they all looked alike. They were the one thing she couldn't do in school.

Marty decided instead to build a circus. She was turning the kitchen table into a lion cage for Wobbly when she looked out the window. There, through a drift of snow near Shirley She-goat's shed, limped a stray cat.

Marty started to call her mom, then stopped. "No cats!" Mom always said.

But more than anything, Marty wanted her very own friend. She poured milk into a bowl. Wobbly watched, tail sweeping the floor.

"Stay, Wobbly!" Marty ordered. Marty opened the door, and Wobbly raced through.

"Eeeow!" the cat cried. He bolted into Shirley's fence, snagging his head in the wire. The cat was thin, like a broken twig. His fur was prickly with cockleburs. Horrible yellow stuff oozed from his eyes. No wonder he couldn't see.

Wobbly was dancing around Marty and her bowl of milk. "You stay in your lion cage!" Marty ordered. She tied Wobbly to a fence post. Then she edged across the yard toward the cat. The snow under Marty's boots crunched. When Marty set down the milk, the cat hissed.

"Fat chance you have of living," Marty whispered at him. "I'm going to name you Chancy." She reached out to pet the cat.

Chancy hissed again. He bared his claws and raked the air. He yanked free. Limping, he ran into the giant elm tree by Marty's house.

"Fat chance you have of making friends," Marty said.

She went inside and sat with Wobbly at the window, watching as Chancy crisscrossed the frozen yard. Finally, Chancy found the bowl of milk. With each gulp, the skin rippled over his ribs.

"Fat chance he has here," Derek said that evening when Marty told him about Chancy. "Mom hates cats."

That night, Marty tossed and turned. She made a plan.

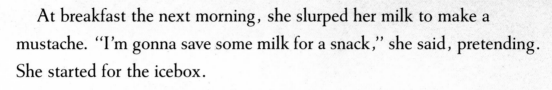

At breakfast the next morning, she slurped her milk to make a mustache. "I'm gonna save some milk for a snack," she said, pretending. She started for the icebox.

"Marty Louise!" Mom said. "Wipe your mouth!"

Marty did just that. Then she hid her mug behind the dill pickles.

"Today, young lady," Mom said, "you are practicing letters."

"I'm training Wobbly Lion," Marty said. "Then I'm feeding my tiger."

As soon as Mom went upstairs, Marty took out Chancy's milk. She went out to Shirley's shed and called Chancy, but he didn't come. She called until her eyes stung with tears.

"Let me see your workbook, dear," Mom said that afternoon.

"I was too busy hunting a tiger," Marty said.

"M is for *Marty*," Mom said. "M has its feet on the floor."

That's silly, Marty thought. She drew her letter with its feet flying.

"That's W with its feet in the air," Mom said. "Like *Wobbly* when you rub her tummy."

"Wobbly won't let me rub her tummy," Marty said.

All week, Marty and Mom disagreed about letters. All week, Marty trained Wobbly for her circus. "Stay, Wobbly Lion," Marty ordered. She snapped her fingers, *whisp*.

On Friday, Marty went out to Shirley's shed. There! Chancy was sitting on a bale of hay inside the shed. Marty crept closer. *Chancy sat on only three legs*. He ran his tongue over the fourth leg, swirling its fur. Marty gasped. That leg was only a stump. It had no paw.

"Fat chance he has anyway," Derek said that night. "Mom hates cats."

A week went by. Two. The crocuses burst out, and the warblers began to sing. Chancy grew plump. His eyes cleared, but still he couldn't see.

In the afternoons, Marty and Derek stayed outside. "You play with your stupid cat," Derek said. He made his fingers go *SNAP*, and Wobbly trotted away after him.

"Chancy," Marty coaxed, peering under Shirley's shed. Nothing. She set out a bowl of milk. Still, Chancy wouldn't come out. But as soon as Marty left, he crept out from under the shed. He drank the milk in his dish and fled.

"Marty, you may have to repeat first grade," Mom said one warm afternoon.

Marty felt empty. She stared at the floor, longing to cradle Chancy against the hollowness in her chest. When Mom left, Marty went in search of Chancy. Wobbly followed her. Marty found Chancy napping on the hay bale.

"Stay, Wobbly Lion," Marty whispered. She snapped her fingers, *whisp.* Then she slipped up and touched Chancy's back.

"EEOW!" Chancy hissed. He bolted out the door of the shed and into the elm.

"Fat chance you have of a petting," Marty said. Her hollowness deepened.

Mom stopped telling Marty to practice her letters. Marty put her
pencils and workbook away. Every morning, Marty visited Shirley, who
was about to kid. One morning, Marty saw Chancy crouching in the
grass. His tail swished. His ears quivered every time Marty took a step.
He pounced on Marty's toes.

"EEEOW!" Marty said. This time she grabbed Chancy.

"EEEEEEEEEEEOW!" Chancy screeched. But Marty held him tight.
Chancy wiggled and squirmed.

"Chancy, Chancy," Marty soothed. She stroked Chancy's back. She
stroked his belly. Chancy sighed. She stroked his ears. Chancy closed
his eyes. She touched his stump. He nuzzled her hand.

"Urrrrrr," he purred.

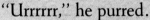

The days grew longer. Marty trained Wobbly Lion to sit. Chancy Tiger learned to circle Marty's ankles. When Shirley She-goat gave birth to twins, Marty added the kids to her circus.

But now Marty was scared because Mom milked Shirley twice a day in the goat shed.

"Fat chance you have of keeping that cat," Derek said. "Mom hates them."

Every morning and evening, just before milking time, Marty coaxed
Chancy away from Shirley's shed. But one Saturday morning, Marty got
too busy watching the baby goats practice their leaps. She was about to
hide Chancy when Mom appeared.

"MARTY LOUISE WHITTSEN!" Mom said.

"Told you so! Told you so!" Derek chanted. He came running,
Wobbly at his heels.

"How often do I have to tell you?" Mom said. "No cats!"

"But Mom, Chancy's my tiger act! He's blind."

"Is not blind," Derek said.

"Is, too!"

"Prove it!"

"Chancy," Marty called.

Chancy lumbered toward Marty. He limped along Shirley's fence. He swerved around the giant elm. He bumped into Wobbly.

"Lie down, Wobbly," Marty ordered. She made her fingers go *SNAP*. Wobbly obeyed.

Chancy nuzzled Wobbly's ears. Wobbly licked his eyes.

"Now that's sweet," Mom said. She held out her hand. "Here, Chancy."

Chancy limped toward Mom. He lifted his stump to her, and then he scrabbled up into her lap.

During those spring days, Chancy slept with Wobbly. At night he slept with Marty, filling the hollow in her chest. The doctor said Marty was almost well enough to go back to school.

"Smarty Marty," Derek said one rainy afternoon. "You'll never write your name!"

"Der-ek," Mom said. "Anyone who tames a tiger can tame a name."

Mom carried Marty and Chancy to her rocking chair. "I know a secret code," she said.

"C, Marty," Mom whispered, petting Chancy's curled back, "C as in courage. C is curved like Chancy Cat."

Mom took Marty's hand, and together they petted Chancy's back in a curving C. Then they petted an A that started at Chancy's nose and stretched out to the tips of his ears. Finally, they tried a T that ran all the way down Chancy's tail.

The next day Marty was painting pictures. Chancy licked his stump.

"Maybe we should paint a circus sign," Marty said.

"Eeow," Chancy said.

Marty painted a clawless C. She sketched a whiskery A. She drew a T with a swishy tail. She held up her painting.

"What do you think?"

Chancy tilted his head. "Eeow," he said.

"Wait 'til you see this one, Fat Chance!"

Marty chose a clean sheet of paper. She selected her favorite brush. Then she set about teaching herself to paint her own name.